In fact, it had rained for so long, that all the Blobs looked as grumbly as Grumbly Green.

Grumbly himself just sat at home and—that's right—grumbled!

Rainbow Blob was happy, too. He was shining brightly with the rainbow in another town—
perhaps *your* town!

...all the colours of the rainbow!
Now Paintbox Land will have a
rainbow in all kinds of weather!"

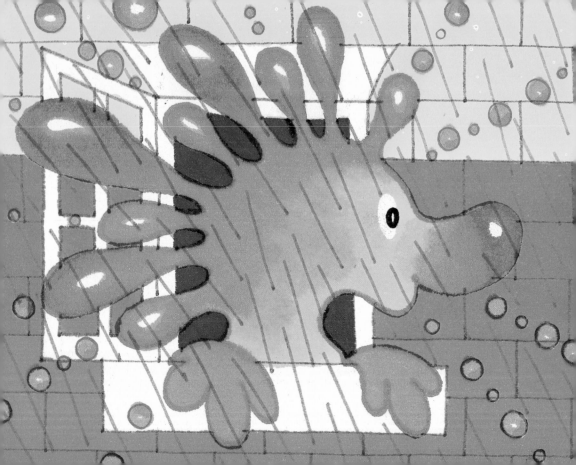

Fizzy Orange fairly fizzed as he looked out of his window.

" Who's been painting my house—red —orange—yellow—green—blue—indigo and violet?" he fizzed.

Then he heard the other Blobs cheering from the street below.

" Rainbow Blob has left us a super surprise," called Royal Blue. " He's painted our houses . . .

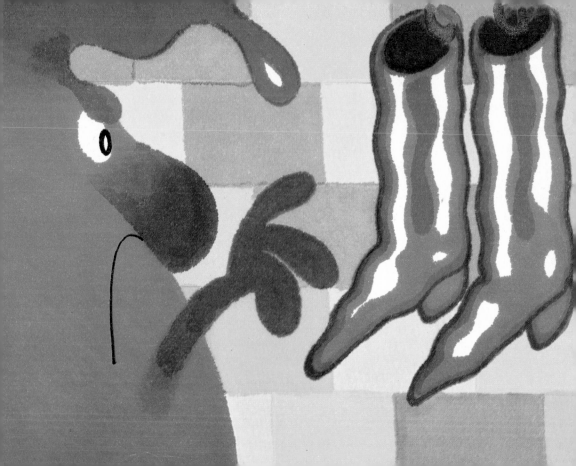

Grumbly Green moaned and groaned as he reached for his pointed wellies.

Pointed wellies? Yes, he needed pointed wellies to fit his pointed feet!

Meanwhile, in the grounds of the palace, Royal Blue blinked as the first drops of rain plopped on his big nose!

" Rainbow Blob's gone—and the rotten rain's on!" he sighed.

Rainbow Blob had almost faded away as he finished his work. `` That's the paint finished . . . '' he whispered.

Even his voice was fading away.

Just what do *you* think his plan was?

Once that was done, he dipped his brush into a pot of orange paint. Then he set to work on the top parts of the walls.

Well, Rainbow Blob had an exciting plan.

He needed a lot of effort—and a lot of paint.

He began by painting the roofs of all the houses a bright red.

Just then, poor Rainbow Blob's colours began to fade, for as you know, rainbows are only seen for a short while.

" I would like to cheer up the Blobs for ever—but I don't have much time left," he said to himself.

Soon, grey clouds covered the sun and the Blobs packed up and went home.

Rainbow Blob looked sadder than anyone. " I don't like to see the other Blobs so unhappy," he sighed.

The Blobs gathered round Royal Blue's radio.

Oh, dear. The weather forecast was nasty . . .

`` The sun will disappear today.
Bright blue skies will turn to grey.
And I forecast, without a doubt,
It's time to get your raincoats out!''
said the voice of the Weather Blob.

But, all too soon a big, grey cloud drifted over the sun.

" Stay away, you spoil-sport cloud!" shouted Rainbow Blob.

Now that the sun was shining, everyone hurried to the beach.

Rainbow Blob glowed brighter than ever because all the other Blobs were so happy.

The Blobs cheered. " It's so nice to see you, Rainbow Blob," said Royal Blue. " It's a shame you can't stay with us for ever."

Then, at last, the rain stopped—and Rainbow Blob appeared.

This very colourful Blob always arrived with the rainbow for a short visit when the sun came out after the rain.